The
Country Life
Book of
NURSERY
RHYMES

Little Miss Muffet,
Who sat on
a Tuffet.

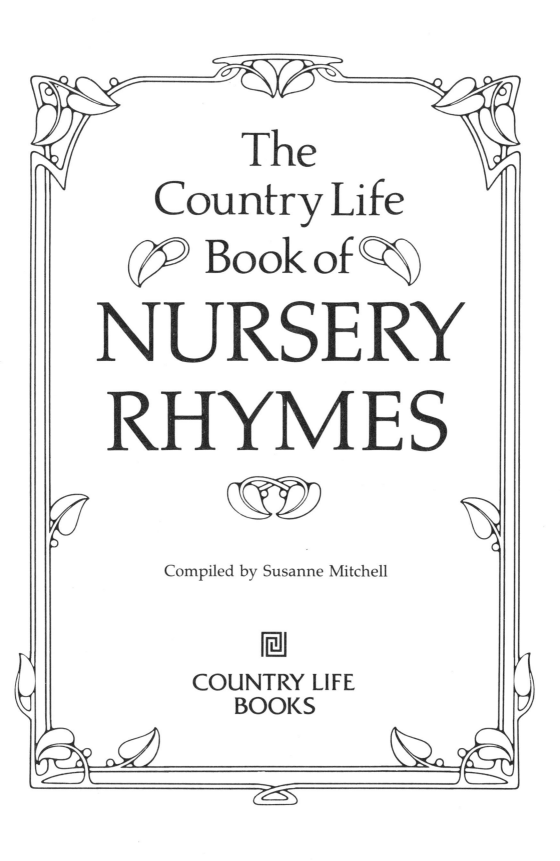

The Country Life Book of

NURSERY RHYMES

Compiled by Susanne Mitchell

COUNTRY LIFE
BOOKS

Frontispiece

Little Miss Muffet. Wellington Hospital, Wellington,
New Zealand

Published by Country Life Books,
an imprint of Newnes Books,
a division of The Hamlyn Publishing Group Limited,
84–88 The Centre, Feltham, Middlesex, England,
and distributed for them by
The Hamlyn Publishing Group Limited,
Rushden, Northants, England.

First published 1984
ISBN 0 600 35728 7
Printed in Italy

Introduction

The Country Life Book of Nursery Rhymes is illustrated with photographs of hand-painted tile pictures depicting a number of the best known nursery rhymes. The tiles were made by Doulton & Co. (now Royal Doulton) between the 1880s and the First World War.

A number of government acts in the 1870s led to extensive hospital building and improvements, which often incorporated children's wards. There emerged a new concern for children's health, which was duly reflected in a wide range of products made by Doulton. These sometimes obscure devices, considered essential for the well-being of children, ranged from small-scale hot-water bottles to water filters. The creation of special children's hospitals and wards stimulated the production of tile murals illustrating nursery rhymes and fairy tales, which were used for their hygienic qualities to decorate the wards and to amuse and cheer the young patients. At the same time Doulton began making the children's tableware for which they are still famous.

The tile pictures, designed by Margaret Thompson, William Rowe and John H. McLennan, were installed in hospitals such as The Royal Victoria Infirmary, Newcastle-upon-Tyne, Buchanan Hospital, St. Leonard's-on-Sea, St. Thomas' Hospital, London, and Wellington Hospital, Wellington, New Zealand – which have been the sources of the illustrations in this book. The tiles were used in many other places throughout Britain and the Empire, some apparently even finding their way to Poona, India.

With the passage of years many of the pictures were unfortunately destroyed, but recent changes in fashion have meant that they are now recognised as works of art in their own right. Some have been restored or resited so that children can, once again, enjoy the intricate detail of these charming pictures whose appeal is as timeless as the stories and rhymes they depict.

The Country Life Book of Nursery Rhymes contains over 200 nursery rhymes, riddles, songs and games that have been played and sung for generations. In fact, for many of us learning nursery rhymes and playing nursery games, such as 'Pat-a-Cake' and 'Round and Round the Garden', introduced us to the intricacies of our language and the craft of reading and writing.

The tile pictures used to illustrate these rhymes appear here for the first time in book form. They are reproduced from specially commissioned colour photographs and show some of the finest examples of Doulton tiles pictures to be seen today. They make *The Country Life Book of Nursery Rhymes* one of the most attractive and unusual anthologies available for children.

S.M.

The
NURSERY
RHYMES

Little Girl, Little Girl

Little girl, little girl, where have you been?
Gathering roses to give to the queen.
Little girl, little girl, what gave she you?
She gave me a diamond as big as my shoe.

Little Miss Muffet

Little Miss Muffet
Who sat on a tuffet,
Eating her curds and whey;
There came a great spider,
Who sat down beside her,
And frightened Miss Muffet away.

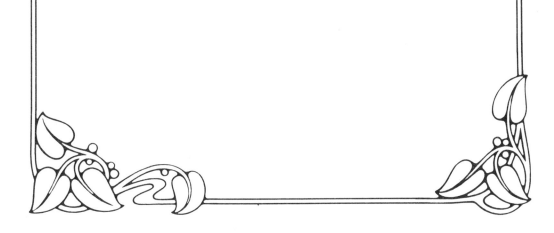

Baa, Baa, Black Sheep

Baa, baa, black sheep,
Have you any wool?
Yes, sir, yes, sir,
Three bags full;
One for my master,
One for my dame,
And one for the little boy
Who lives down the lane.

Bless you,
Bless you, Burnie Bee

Bless you, bless you, burnie bee:
Say, when will your wedding be?
If it be to-morrow day,
Take your wings and fly away.

A was an Apple Pie

A was an apple pie;
B bit it,
C cut it,
D dealt it,
E ate it,
F fought for it,
G got it,
H had it,
I inspected it,
J jumped for it,
K kept it,
L longed for it,
M mourned for it,
N nodded at it,
O opened it,
P peeped in it,
Q quartered it,
R ran for it,
S stole it,
T took it,
U upset it,
V viewed it,
W wanted it,
X, Y, Z and ampersand
All wished for a piece in hand.

Bye Baby Bunting

Bye baby bunting,
Father's gone a hunting,
To get a little rabbit-skin,
To wrap his little baby in.

Hush Little Baby

Hush, little baby, don't say a word,
Papa's going to buy you a mocking bird.

If the mocking bird won't sing,
Papa's going to buy you a diamond ring.

If the diamond ring turns to brass,
Papa's going to buy you a looking-glass.

If the looking-glass gets broke,
Papa's going to buy you a billy-goat.

If that billy-goat runs away,
Papa's going to buy you another today.

I See the Moon

I see the moon,
And the moon sees me;
God bless the moon,
And God bless me.

A Frog He Would A-Wooing Go

A frog he would a-wooing go,
Heigho, says Rowley,
Whether his mother would let him or no.
With a rowley, powley, gammon and spinach,
Heigho, says Anthony Rowley.

So off he set with his opera hat,
Heigho, says Rowley,
And on the road he met with a rat.
With a rowley, powley, gammon and spinach,
Heigho, says Anthony Rowley.

'Pray, Mr Rat, will you go with me?'
Heigho, says Rowley,
'Kind Mrs Mousey for to see?'
With a rowley, powley, gammon and spinach,
Heigho, says Anthony Rowley.

They came to the door of Mousey's hall,
Heigho, says Rowley,
They gave a loud knock and they gave a loud call.
With a rowley, powley, gammon and spinach,
Heigho, says Anthony Rowley.

'Pray, Mrs Mouse, are you within?'
Heigho, says Rowley,
'Oh, yes, kind sirs, I'm sitting to spin.'
With a rowley, powley, gammon and spinach,
Heigho, says Anthony Rowley.

'Pray, Mrs Mouse, will you give us some beer?'
Heigho, says Rowley,
'For Froggy and I are fond of good cheer.'
With a rowley, powley, gammon and spinach,
Heigho, says Anthony Rowley.

'Pray, Mr Frog, will you give us a song?'
Heigho, says Rowley,
'But let it be something that's not very long.'
With a rowley, powley, gammon and spinach,
Heigho, says Anthony Rowley.

'Indeed, Mrs Mouse,' replied the frog,
Heigho, says Rowley,
'A cold has made me as hoarse as a dog,'
With a rowley, powley, gammon and spinach,
Heigho, says Anthony Rowley.

'Since you have caught cold, Mr Frog,' Mousey said,
Heigho, says Rowley,
'I'll sing you a song that I have just made.'
With a rowley, powley, gammon and spinach,
Heigho, says Anthony Rowley.

But while they were all a merry-making,
Heigho, says Rowley,
A cat and her kittens came tumbling in.
With a rowley, powley, gammon and spinach,
Heigho, says Anthony Rowley.

The cat she seized the rat by the crown;
Heigho, says Rowley,
The kittens they pulled the little mouse down.
With a rowley, powley, gammon and spinach,
Heigho, says Anthony Rowley.

This put Mr Frog in a terrible fright,
Heigho, says Rowley,
He took up his hat, and he wished them goodnight.
With a rowley, powley, gammon and spinach,
Heigho, says Anthony Rowley.

But as Froggy was crossing over a brook,
Heigho, says Rowley,
A lily-white duck came and gobbled him up.
With a rowley, powley, gammon and spinach,
Heigho, says Anthony Rowley.

So there was an end of one, two, and three,
Heigho, says Rowley,
The rat, the mouse, and the little frog-gee!
With a rowley, powley, gammon and spinach,
Heigho, says Anthony Rowley.

Little Boy Jack

Once a little boy, Jack, was, oh! ever so good,
Till he took a strange notion to cry all he could.

So he cried all the day, and he cried all the night,
He cried in the morning and in the twilight;

He cried till his voice was as hoarse as a crow,
And his mouth grew so large it looked like a great O.

It grew at the bottom, and grew at the top;
It grew till they thought that it would never stop.

Each day his great mouth grew taller and taller,
And his dear little self grew smaller and smaller.

At last, that same mouth grew so big that – alack! –
It was only a mouth with a border of Jack.

Catkin

I have a little pussy,
And her coat is silver grey;
She lives in a great wide meadow
And she never runs away.
She always is a pussy,
She'll never be a cat
Because – she's a pussy willow!
Now what do you think of that!

Blow, Wind, Blow

Blow, wind, blow, and go, mill, go,
That the miller may grind his corn;
That the baker may take it,
And into bread make it,
And bring us a loaf in the morn.

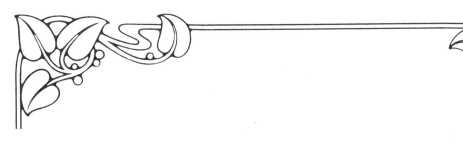

Daffy-Down-Dilly

Daffy-down-dilly is new come to town,
With a yellow petticoat, and a green gown.

Over in the Meadow

Over in the meadow in the sand in the sun
Lived an old mother turtle and her little turtle – one.
'Dig,' said the mother. 'We dig,' said the one,
So they dug all day in the sand in the sun.

Over in the meadow where the stream runs blue
Lived an old mother fish and her little fishes – two.
'Swim,' said the mother. 'We swim,' said the two,
So they swam all day where the stream runs blue.

Over in the meadow in a hole in a tree
Lived an old mother owl and her little owls – three.
'Tu-whoo,' said the mother. 'Tu-whoo,' said the three,
So they tu-whooed all day in a hole in a tree.

Over in the meadow by the old barn door
Lived an old mother rat and her little ratties – four.
'Gnaw,' said the mother. 'We gnaw,' said the four,
So they gnawed all day by the old barn door.

Over in the meadow in a snug beehive
Lived an old mother bee and her little bees – five.
'Buzz,' said the mother. 'We buzz,' said the five,
So they buzzed all day in a snug beehive.

Over in the meadow in a nest built of sticks
Lived an old mother crow and her little crows – six.
'Caw,' said the mother. 'We caw,' said the six,
So they cawed all day in a nest built of sticks.

Over in the meadow where the grass grows so even
Lived an old mother frog and her little froggies – seven.
'Jump,' said the mother. 'We jump,' said the seven,
So they jumped all day where the grass grows so even.

Over in the meadow by the old mossy gate
Lived an old mother lizard and her little lizards – eight.
'Bask,' said the mother. 'We bask,' said the eight,
So they basked all day by the old mossy gate.

Over in the meadow by the old scotch pine
Lived an old mother duck and her little ducks – nine.
'Quack,' said the mother. 'We quack,' said the nine,
So they quacked all day by the old scotch pine.

Over in the meadow in a cosy wee den
Lived an old mother beaver and her little beavers – ten.
'Beave,' said the mother. 'We beave,' said the ten,
So they beaved all day in a cosy wee den.

In a Cottage in Fife

In a cottage in Fife
Lived a man and his wife,
Who, believe me, were comical folk;
For, to people's surprise,
They both saw with their eyes,
And their tongues moved whenever they spoke.
When quite fast asleep,
I've been told that to keep
Their eyes open they could not contrive;
They walked on their feet,
And 'twas thought what they eat
Helped, with drinking, to keep them alive.

Nellie Bligh

Nellie Bligh caught a fly
Going home from school.
Put it in a hot mince pie,
Waiting by to cool.

Georgie Porgie

Georgie Porgie, pudding and pie,
Kissed the girls and made them cry;
When the boys came out to play,
Georgie Porgie ran away.

The Man in the Wilderness

The man in the wilderness asked of me
How many strawberries grew in the sea?
I answered him, as I thought good,
'As many red herrings as grow in the wood.'

A Tisket, a Tasket

A tisket, a tasket,
A green and yellow basket,
I wrote a letter to my love,
And on the way I dropped it.
I dropped it,
I dropped it,
And on the way I dropped it.
A little boy picked it up
And put it in his pocket.

The Fat Man of Bombay

There was a fat man of Bombay,
Who was smoking one sunshiny day,
When a bird called a snipe
Flew away with his pipe,
Which vexed the fat man of Bombay.

Who Killed Cock Robin?

Who killed Cock Robin?
'I,' said the sparrow,
'With my bow and arrow,
I killed Cock Robin.'

Who saw him die?
'I,' said the fly,
'With my little eye,
I saw him die.'

Who caught his blood?
'I,' said the fish,
'With my little dish,
I caught his blood.'

Who'll make his shroud?
'I,' said the beetle,
'With my thread and needle,
I'll make his shroud.'

Who'll dig his grave?
'I,' said the owl,
'With my spade and trowel,
I'll dig his grave.'

Who'll be the clerk?
'I,' said the lark,
'If it's not in the dark,
I'll be the clerk.'

Who'll be the parson?
'I,' said the rook,
'With my little book,
I'll be the parson.'

Who'll sing a psalm?
'I,' said the thrush,
As she sat on a bush,
'I'll sing a psalm.'

Who'll be chief mourner?
'I,' said the dove,
'I mourn for my love,
I'll be chief mourner.'

Who'll toll the bell?
'I,' said the bull,
'Because I can pull,
I'll toll the bell.'

All the birds of the air
Fell sighing and sobbing,
When they heard the bell toll
For poor Cock Robin.

To all it concerns,
This notice apprises,
The sparrow's for trial
At next bird assizes.

Ding, Dong, Bell

Ding, dong, bell,
Pussy's in the well.
Who put her in?
Little Johnny Green.
Who pulled her out?
Little Johnny Stout.
What a naughty boy was that
To try to drown poor pussy cat,
Which never did him any harm,
But killed the mice in his father's barn.

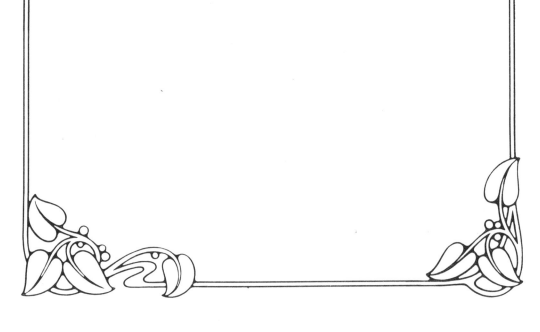

Goosey

Goosey Gander.

Goosey, Goosey Gander

Goosey, goosey gander,
Whither shall I wander?
Upstairs and downstairs
And in my lady's chamber.
There I met an old man
Who would not say his prayers,
I took him by his left leg
And threw him down the stairs.

A Year in the Country

January brings the snow,
Makes our feet and fingers glow.

February brings the rain,
Thaws the frozen lake again.

March brings breezes loud and shrill,
Stirs the dancing daffodil.

April brings the primrose sweet,
Scatters daisies at our feet.

May brings flocks of pretty lambs,
Skipping by their fleecy dams.

June brings tulips, lilies, roses,
Fills the children's hands with posies.

Hot July brings cooling showers,
Apricots and gillyflowers.

August brings the sheaves of corn,
Then the harvest home is borne.

Warm September brings the fruit,
Sportsmen then begin to shoot.

Fresh October brings the pheasant,
Then to gather nuts is pleasant.

Dull November brings the blast,
Then the leaves are whirling fast.

Chill December brings the sleet,
Blazing fire, and Christmas treat.

As I Went Down to Derby Town

As I went down to Derby town,
'Twas on a market day,
And there I met the finest ram
That was ever fed on hay.

The wool upon this ram's back,
It grew up to the sky;
The eagles built their nests in it,
I heard the young ones cry.

The horns upon this ram's head,
They grew up to the moon.
A man climbed up in April
And never came down till June.

This ram he had four mighty feet
And on them he did stand,
And every foot that he had got
Did cover an acre of land.

And if you don't believe me
And think it is a lie,
Then you go down to Derby town
And see as well as I.

One He Loves

One he loves,
Two, he loves,
Three, he loves, they say.
Four, he loves with all his heart;
And five, he casts away.
Six, he loves,
Seven she loves,
Eight, they both love.
Nine, he comes,
Ten, he tarries;
Eleven, he courts,
Twelve, he marries.

Jack's House

This is the house that Jack built.

This is the malt
That lay in the house that Jack built.

This is the rat
That ate the malt
That lay in the house that Jack built.

This is the cat
That killed the rat
That ate the malt
That lay in the house that Jack built.

This is the dog
That worried the cat
That killed the rat
That ate the malt
That lay in the house that Jack built.

This is the cow with the crumpled horn,
That tossed the dog
That worried the cat
That killed the rat
That ate the malt
That lay in the house that Jack built.

This is the maiden all forlorn,
That milked the cow with the crumpled horn,
That tossed the dog
That worried the cat
That killed the rat
That ate the malt
That lay in the house that Jack built.

This is the man all tattered and torn,
That kissed the maiden all forlorn,
That milked the cow with the crumpled horn,
That tossed the dog
That worried the cat
That killed the rat
That ate the malt
That lay in the house that Jack built.

This is the priest all shaven and shorn,
That married the man all tattered and torn,
That kissed the maiden all forlorn,
That milked the cow with the crumpled horn,
That tossed the dog
That worried the cat
That killed the rat
That ate the malt
That lay in the house that Jack built.

This is the cock that crowed in the morn,
That waked the priest all shaven and shorn,
That married the man all tattered and torn,
That kissed the maiden all forlorn,
That milked the cow with the crumpled horn,
That tossed the dog
That worried the cat
That killed the rat
That ate the malt
That lay in the house that Jack built.

This is the farmer sowing the corn,
That kept the cock that crowed in the morn,
That waked the priest all shaven and shorn,
That married the man all tattered and torn,
That kissed the maiden all forlorn,
That milked the cow with the crumpled horn,
That tossed the dog
That worried the cat
That killed the rat
That ate the malt
That lay in the house that Jack built.

I Had a Little Hen

I had a little hen,
The prettiest ever seen;
She washed up the dishes,
And kept the house clean.
She went to the mill
To fetch some flour,
And always got home
In less than an hour;
She baked me my bread,
She brewed me my ale;
She sat by the fire
And told a fine tale.

As I Walked by Myself

As I walked by myself
And talked to myself,
Myself said unto me,
'Look to thyself,
Take care of thyself,
For nobody cares for thee.'

I answered myself
And said to myself,
In the selfsame repartee,
'Look to thyself
Or not to thyself,
The selfsame thing will be.'

Hark, Hark

Hark, hark,
The dogs do bark,
The beggars are coming to town;
Some in rags,
And some in jags,
And one in a velvet gown.

Hickory, Dickory, Dock

Hickory, dickory, dock,
The mouse ran up the clock.
The clock struck one,
The mouse ran down,
Hickory, dickory, dock.

Chinese Sandmen

Chinese Sandmen,
Wise and creepy,
Croon dream songs
To make us sleepy.
A Chinese maid with slanting eyes
Is queen of all their lullabies.
On her ancient moon-guitar
She strums a sleep song to a star;
And when big China shadows fall
Snow-white lilies hear her call.
Chinese Sandmen,
Wise and creepy,
Croon dream songs
To make us sleepy.

Matthew, Mark, Luke and John

Matthew, Mark, Luke and John,
Bless the bed that I lie on.
All four corners round about,
When I get in, when I get out.

Four corners to my bed,
Four angels round my head;
One to watch and one to pray,
And two to bear my soul away.

Twinkle, Twinkle, Little Star

Twinkle, twinkle, little star,
How I wonder what you are.
Up above the world so high,
Like a diamond in the sky.

When the blazing sun is gone,
When he nothing shines upon,
Then you show your little light,
Twinkle, twinkle, all the night.

Then the traveller in the dark,
Thanks you for your tiny spark,
How could he see where to go,
If you did not twinkle so?

In the dark blue sky you keep,
And often through my curtains peep,
For you never shut your eye,
'Till the sun is in the sky.

As your bright and tiny spark,
Lights the traveller in the dark,
Though I know not what you are,
Twinkle, twinkle, little star.

Where Are You Going, My Pretty Maid?

'Where are you going, my pretty maid?'
'I'm going a-milking, sir,' she said.

'May I go with you, my pretty maid?'
'You're kindly welcome, sir,' she said.

'What is your father, my pretty maid?'
'My father's a farmer, sir,' she said.

'What is your fortune, my pretty maid?'
'My face is my fortune, sir,' she said.

'Then I can't marry you, my pretty maid.'
'Nobody asked you, sir,' she said.

The Owl and the Eel

The owl and the eel and the warming pan,
They went to call on the soap-fat man.
The soap-fat man, he was not within,
He'd gone for a ride on his rolling-pin.
So they all came back by the way of the town,
And turned the meeting-house upside down.

Bow, Wow, Wow

Bow, wow, wow,
Whose dog art thou?
Little Tom Tinker's dog,
Bow, wow, wow.

Curly Locks

Curly locks, Curly locks,
Wilt thou be mine?
Thou shalt not wash dishes,
Nor yet feed the swine;
But sit on a cushion,
And saw a fine seam,
And feed upon strawberries,
Sugar and cream.

Three Little Ghostesses

Three little ghostesses
Sitting on postesses
Eating buttered toastesses,
And greasing their fistesses
Right up to their wristesses.
Weren't they beastesses
To make such feastesses!

Pease Pudding

Pease pudding hot,
Pease pudding cold,
Pease pudding in the pot,
Nine days old.

Some like it hot,
Some like it cold,
Some like it in the pot,
Nine days old.

Wee Willie Winkie

Wee Willie Winkie runs through the town,
Upstairs and downstairs in his nightgown,
Rapping at the window, crying through the lock,
'Are the children in their beds, for now it's eight o'clock?'

Star Light, Star Bright

Star light, star bright,
First star I've seen tonight,
I wish I may, I wish I might,
Have the wish I wish tonight.

Go to Bed First

Go to bed first, a golden purse;
Go to bed second, a golden pheasant;
Go to bed third, a golden bird.

A Farmer Went Trotting

A farmer went trotting upon his grey mare,
Bumpety, bumpety, bump!
With his daughter behind him so rosy and fair,
Lumpety, lumpety, lump!

A raven cried 'Croak!' and they all tumbled down,
Bumpety, bumpety, bump!
The mare broke her knees and the farmer his crown,
Lumpety, lumpety, lump!

The mischievous raven flew laughing away.
Bumpety, bumpety, bump!
And vowed he would serve them the same the next day,
Lumpety, lumpety, lump!

A Needle and Thread

Old Mother Twitchett had but one eye,
And a long tail which she let fly;
And every time she went through a gap,
She left a bit of her tail in a trap.

Hush-a-bye, Baby

Hush-a-bye, baby, on the tree top,
When the wind blows the cradle will rock;
When the bough breaks the cradle will fall,
Down will come baby, cradle, and all.

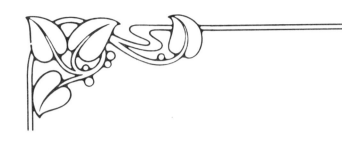

I Had a Little Husband

I had a little husband,
No bigger than my thumb;
I put him in a pint pot,
And there I bid him drum.

I gave him some garters,
To garter up his hose,
And a little handkerchief
To wipe his pretty nose.

I bought a little horse,
That galloped up and down;
I bridled him, and saddled him,
And sent him out of town.

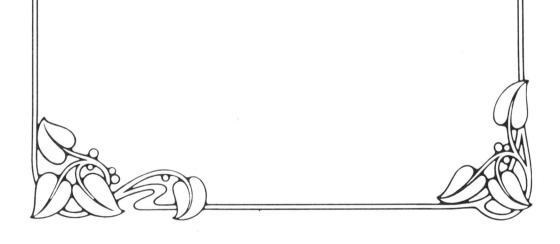

I Saw a Peacock

I saw a peacock with a fiery tail
I saw a blazing comet drop down hail
I saw a cloud wrapped with ivy round
I saw a sturdy oak creep on the ground
I saw a pismire swallow up a whale
I saw a raging sea brimful of ale
I saw a Venice glass sixteen foot deep
I saw a well full of men's tears that weep
I saw their eyes all in a flame of fire
I saw a house as big as the moon and higher
I saw the sun even in the midst of night
I saw the man that saw this wondrous sight.

Pat-a-Cake

Pat-a-cake, pat-a-cake, baker's man,
Bake me a cake as fast as you can;
Roll it and pat it and mark it with 'B',
And put it in the oven for baby and me.

Ride a Cock-horse

Ride a cock-horse to Banbury Cross,
To see a fine lady upon a white horse;
Rings on her fingers and bells on her toes,
She shall have music wherever she goes.

A Star

I have a little sister, they call her Peep-peep,
She wades the waters, deep, deep, deep;
She climbs the mountains high, high, high;
Poor little creature, she has but one eye.

Three Wise Men of Gotham

Three wise men of Gotham
Went to sea in a bowl;
If the bowl had been stronger,
My song would have been longer.

If All the Seas Were One Sea

If all the seas were one sea,
What a great sea that would be!
If all the trees were one tree,
What a great tree that would be!
If all the axes were one axe,
What a great axe that would be!
And if all the men were one man,
What a great man that would be!
And if the great man took the great axe
And cut down the great tree
And let it fall into the great sea,
What a splish-splash that would be!

Round the Rugged Rock

Round and round the rugged rock
The ragged rascal ran,
How many R's are there in that?
Now tell me if you can.

Red Sky at Night

Red sky at night,
Shepherd's delight;
Red sky in the morning,
Shepherd's warning.

Peter Piper

Peter Piper picked a peck of pickled pepper;
A peck of pickled pepper Peter Piper picked.
If Peter Piper picked a peck of pickled pepper,
Where's the peck of pickled pepper Peter Piper picked?

If All the World

If all the world were paper,
And all the sea were ink,
If all the trees were bread and cheese,
What should we have to drink?

Sneeze on Monday

Sneeze on Monday, sneeze for danger,
Sneeze on Tuesday, kiss a stranger,
Sneeze on Wednesday, get a letter,
Sneeze on Thursday, something better,
Sneeze on Friday, sneeze for sorrow,
Sneeze on Saturday, see your sweetheart to-morrow.

For the Want of a Nail

For the want of a nail, the shoe was lost,
For the want of a shoe, the horse was lost,
For the want of a horse, the rider was lost,
For the want of a rider, the battle was lost,
For the want of a battle, the kingdom was lost,
And all for the want of a horseshoe nail.

As I Was Going to St Ives

As I was going to St Ives,
I met a man with seven wives.
Each wife had seven sacks,
Each sack had seven cats,
Each cat had seven kits;
Kits, cats, sacks and wives,
How many were going to St Ives?

The North Wind

The north wind doth blow,
And we shall have snow,
And what will poor robin do then, poor thing?
He'll sit in a barn,
And keep himself warm,
And hide his head under his wing, poor thing.

The north wind doth blow,
And we shall have snow,
And what will the swallow do then, poor thing?
O, do you not know,
He's gone long ago
To a country much warmer than ours, poor thing?

The north wind doth blow,
And we shall have snow,
And what will the dormouse do then, poor thing?
Rolled up in a ball,
In his nest snug and small,
He'll sleep till the winter is past, poor thing.

The north wind doth blow,
And we shall have snow,
And what will the children do then, poor things?
O, when lessons are done,
They'll jump, skip, and run,
And play till they make themselves warm, poor things.

St Swithin's Day

St Swithin's day, if thou dost rain,
For forty days it will remain;
St Swithin's day, if thou be fair,
For forty days 't will rain na mair.

Rain, Rain

Rain, rain, go away,
Come again another day;
Little Tommy wants to play.

Old Peg

There was an old woman, her name it was Peg;
Her head was of wood and she wore a cork leg.
The neighbours all pitched her into the water,
Her leg was drowned first, and her head followed after.

It's Raining, It's Pouring

It's raining, it's pouring,
The old man is snoring;
He got into bed and bumped his head
And couldn't get up in the morning.

I Saw a Ship A-sailing

I saw a ship a-sailing,
A-sailing on the sea;
And, oh! it was all laden
With pretty things for thee!

There were comfits in the cabin,
And apples in the hold;
The sails were made of silk,
And the masts were made of gold.

The four-and-twenty sailors
That stood between the decks,
Were four-and-twenty white mice,
With chains about their necks.

The captain was a duck,
With a packet on his back;
And when the ship began to move,
The captain said, 'Quack! quack!'

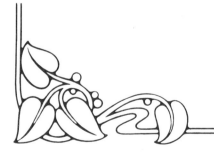

I saw a ship a-sailing,

Jack fell down
And broke his crown,
And Jill came
tumbling after.

Jack and Jill

Jack and Jill went up the hill
To fetch a pail of water;
Jack fell down, and broke his crown,
And Jill came tumbling after.

Then up Jack got, and home did trot,
As fast as he could caper,
To old Dame Dob, who patched his nob
With vinegar and brown paper.

Then Jill came in, and she did grin,
To see Jack's paper plaster;
Her mother, vexed, did whip her next,
For laughing at Jack's disaster.

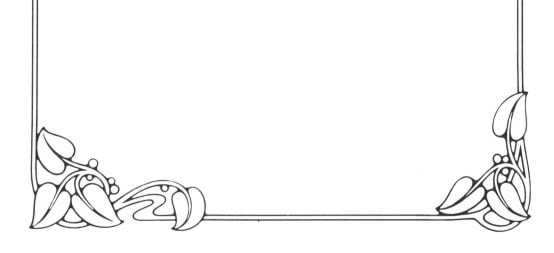

Monday's Child

Monday's child is fair of face,
Tuesday's child is full of grace,
Wednesday's child is full of woe,
Thursday's child has far to go,
Friday's child is loving and giving,
Saturday's child works hard for a living,
And the child that is born on the Sabbath day
Is bonny and blithe, and good and gay.

Finger-nails

Cut them on Monday, you cut them for health,
Cut them on Tuesday, you cut them for wealth,
Cut them on Wednesday, you cut them for news,
Cut them on Thursday, a new pair of shoes,
Cut them on Friday, you cut them for sorrow,
Cut them on Saturday, see your true love to-morrow,
Cut them on Sunday, ill luck will be with you all the week.

Christmas Is Coming

Christmas is coming, the geese are getting fat;
Please to put a penny in the old man's hat;
If you haven't got a penny, ha'penny will do.
If you haven't got a ha'penny, God bless you.

Tom, He Was a Piper's Son

Tom, he was a piper's son,
He learned to play when he was young,
And all the tune that he could play
Was, 'Over the hills and far away';
Over the hills and a great way off,
The wind shall blow my top-knot off.

Now, Tom with his pipe made such a noise,
That he pleased both the girls and boys,
And they all stopped to hear him play,
'Over the hills and far away.'

Tom with his pipe did play with such skill
That those who heard him could never keep still;
As soon as he played they began to dance,
Even pigs on their hind legs would after him prance.

As Dolly was milking her cow one day,
Tom took his pipe and began to play;
So Doll and the cow danced 'The Cheshire Round',
Till the pail was broken and the milk ran on the ground.

He met old Dame Trot with a basket of eggs,
He used his pipe and she used her legs;
She danced about till the eggs were all broke,
She began for to fret, but he laughed at the joke.

Tom saw a cross fellow was beating an ass,
Heavy laden with pots, pans, dishes, and glass;
He took out his pipe and played them a tune,
And the poor donkey's load was lightened full soon.

The Rose Is Red

The rose is red, the violet blue,
The gillyflower sweet, and so are you.
These are the words you bade me say
For a pair of new gloves on Easter day.

Dame, Get Up

Dame, get up and bake your pies,
Bake your pies, bake your pies;
Dame, get up and bake your pies,
On Christmas Day in the morning.

Dame, what makes your maidens lie,
Maidens lie, maidens lie;
Dame, what makes your maidens lie,
On Christmas Day in the morning?

Dame, what makes your ducks to die,
Ducks to die, ducks to die;
Dame, what makes your ducks to die,
On Christmas Day in the morning?

Their wings are cut, and they cannot fly,
Cannot fly, cannot fly;
Their wings are cut, and they cannot fly,
On Christmas Day in the morning.

The Miller He Grinds His Corn

The miller he grinds his corn, his corn;
The miller he grinds his corn, his corn;
The little boy blue comes winding his horn,
With a hop, step, and a jump.

The carter he whistles aside his team,
The carter he whistles aside his team;
And Dolly comes tripping with nice thick cream,
With a hop, step, and a jump.

The nightingale sings when we are at rest,
The nightingale sings when we are at rest;
The little bird climbs the tree for his nest,
With a hop, step, and a jump.

The damsels are churning for curds and whey,
The damsels are churning for curds and whey,
The lads in the field are making the hay,
With a hop, step, and a jump.

Moses

Moses supposes his toeses are roses,
But Moses supposes erroneously;
For nobody's toeses are posies of roses
As Moses supposes his toeses to be.

There Was a Little Woman

There was a little woman,
As I've heard tell,
She went to market
Her eggs for to sell;
She went to market
All on a market day,
And she fell asleep
On the king's highway.

There came by a pedlar
Whose name was Stout,
He cut her petticoats
All round about;
He cut her petticoats
Up to her knees;
Which made the little woman
To shiver and sneeze.

When this little woman
Began to awake,
She began to shiver,
And she began to shake;
She began to shake,
And she began to cry,
'Lawk-a-mercy on me,
This is none of I!'

'But if this be I,
As I do hope it be,
I have a little dog at home
And he'll know me;
If it be I,
He'll wag his little tail,
And if it be not I
He'll loudly bark and wail!'

Home went the little woman
All in the dark,
Up got the little dog,
And he began to bark;
He began to bark,
And she began to cry,
'Lawk-a-mercy on me,
This is none of I!'

There Was a Man and He Had Nought

There was a man and he had nought,
And robbers came to rob him;
He crept up to the chimney top,
And then they thought they had him.

But he got down on t' other side,
And then they could not find him;
He ran fourteen miles in fifteen days,
And never looked behind him.

Little Bo-Peep

Little Bo-peep has lost her sheep,
And can't tell where to find them;
Leave them alone, and they'll come home,
Bringing their tails behind them.

Little Bo-peep fell fast asleep,
And dreamt she heard them bleating;
But when she awoke, she found it a joke,
For they were still all fleeting.

Then up she took her little crook,
Determined for to find them;
She found them indeed, but it made her heart bleed,
For they'd left their tails behind them.

It happened one day, as Bo-peep did stray
Into a meadow hard by,
There she espied their tails side by side,
All hung on a tree to dry.

Little Bo-Peep

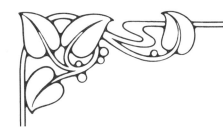

Little Boy Blue

Little Boy Blue,
Come blow your horn,
The sheep's in the meadow,
The cow's in the corn.

But where is the boy
Who looks after the sheep?
He's under a haycock,
Fast asleep.

'Will you wake him?'
'No, not I,
For if I do,
He's sure to cry.'

There Was a Man,
He Went Mad

There was a man and he went mad,
He jumped into a paper bag;
The paper bag was too narrow,
He jumped into a wheelbarrow;
The wheelbarrow took on fire,
He jumped into a cow byre;
The cow byre was too nasty,
He jumped into an apple pasty;
The apple pasty was too sweet,
He jumped into Chester-le-Street;
Chester-le-Street was full of stones,
He fell down and broke his bones.

I saw an Old Man

I saw an old man put shells in his pocket,
And up to the sky he went like a rocket;
But what he did there I could not but wonder,
As while I yet looked I thought I heard thunder.

'Old fellow, old fellow, old fellow,' cried I,
'Oh whither, oh whither, oh whither so high?'
'The moon is green cheese, which I go to bring.
One half is for you, the rest for the king!'

Sulky Sue

Here's Sulky Sue,
What shall we do?
Turn her face to the wall
Till she comes to.

Old Mother Shuttle

Old Mother Shuttle
Lived in a coal scuttle
Along with her dog and her cat.
What they ate I can't tell,
But it's known very well,
That none of the party was fat.

Old Mother Shuttle
Scoured out her coal scuttle,
And washed both her dog and her cat.
The cat scratched her nose,
So they came to hard blows,
And who was the gainer by that?

Cobbler, Cobbler

Cobbler, cobbler, mend my shoe,
Get it done by half-past two.
Half-past two is much too late,
Get it done by half-past eight.

Lucy Locket

Lucy Locket lost her pocket,
Kitty Fisher found it;
There was not a penny in it,
But a ribbon round it.

Little Tommy Tucker

Little Tommy Tucker,
Sings for his supper.
What shall we give him?
White bread and butter.
How shall he cut it
Without a knife?
How will he be married
Without a wife?

When I Was a Little Boy

When I was a little boy
I had but little wit;
It is some time ago,
And I have no more yet;
Nor ever, ever shall
Until that I die,
For the longer I live
The more fool am I.

Jack, Be Nimble

Jack be nimble,
Jack be quick,
Jack jump over the candlestick.

Up at Piccadilly, Oh!

Up at Piccadilly, oh!
The coachman takes his stand,
And when he meets a pretty girl
He takes her by the hand;
Whip away forever, oh!
Drive away so clever, oh!
All the way to Bristol, oh!
He drives her four-in-hand.

Tweedle-dum and Tweedle-dee

Tweedle-dum and Tweedle-dee
Went down to have a battle,
For Tweedle-dum said Tweedle-dee
Had spoiled his nice new rattle.
Just then flew by a monstrous crow,
As big as a tar-barrel,
Which frightened both the heroes so,
They quite forgot their quarrel.

Nothing-at-all

There was an old woman called Nothing-at-all,
Who lived in a dwelling exceedingly small;
A man stretched his mouth to its utmost extent,
And down in one gulp, house and old woman went.

Gregory Griggs

Gregory Griggs, Gregory Griggs,
Had twenty-seven different wigs.
He wore them up, he wore them down,
To please the people of the town;
He wore them east, he wore them west,
But he never could tell which he liked best.

One Misty, Moisty Morning

One misty, moisty morning,
When cloudy was the weather,
I chanced to meet an old man
Clothed all in leather;
He began to compliment,
And I began to grin,
'How do you do?' and 'How do you do?'
And 'How do you do?' again!

Little Jack Horner

Little Jack Horner
Sat in the corner,
Eating a Christmas pie;
He put in a thumb,
And pulled out a plum,
And said, 'What a good boy am I.'

Three Men in a Tub

Rub-a-dub-dub,
Three men in a tub;
And who do you think they be?
The butcher, the baker,
The candlestick-maker;
They all jumped out of a rotten potato,
'Twas enough to make a man stare.

Little Polly Flinders

Little Polly Flinders
Sat among the cinders,
Warming her pretty little toes.
Her mother came and caught her,
And whipped her little daughter,
For spoiling her nice new clothes.

Here Is the Church

Here is the church, and here is the steeple;
Open the door and here are the people.
Here is the parson going upstairs,
And here he is a-saying his prayers.

The Man in the Moon

The man in the moon
Came down too soon,
And asked his way to Norwich;
He went by the south,
And burnt his mouth
With eating cold plum porridge.

Don't Care

Don't Care didn't care,
Don't Care was wild:
Don't Care stole plum and pear
Like any beggar's child.

Don't Care was made to care,
Don't Care was hung:
Don't Care was put in a pot
And boiled till he was done.

There Was a Maid

There was a maid on Scrabble Hill,
And if.not dead, she lives there still;
She grew so tall, she reached the sky,
And on the moon, hung clothes to dry.

There Was a Crooked Man

There was a crooked man, and he went a crooked mile,
He found a crooked sixpence against a crooked stile,
He bought a crooked cat, which caught a crooked mouse,
And they all lived together in a little crooked house.

Girls and Boys

Girls and boys, come out to play,
The moon is shining bright as day;
Leave your supper and leave your sleep,
And come with your playfellows into the street;
Come with a whoop and come with a call,
Come with a good will, or come not at all.
Up the ladder and down the wall,
A ha'penny loaf will serve us all:
You find milk and I'll find flour,
And we'll have a pudding in half-an-hour.

The Crocodile

If you should meet a crocodile
Don't take a stick and poke him.
Ignore the welcome in his smile,
Be careful not to stroke him.
For as he sleeps upon the Nile,
He thinner gets and thinner;
So whene'er you meet a crocodile
He's ready for his dinner.

As I Was Going Out

As I was going out one day
My head fell off and rolled away.
But when I saw that it was gone,
I picked it up and put it on.

And when I got into the street
A fellow cried, 'Look at your feet!'
I looked at them and sadly said,
'I've left them both asleep in bed!'

Mother, May I Go to Swim?

Mother, may I go to swim?
Yes, my darling daughter.
Fold your clothes up neat and trim,
But don't go near the water.

Bobby Shaftoe

Bobby Shaftoe's gone to sea,
Silver buckles on his knee;
He'll come back and marry me,
Bonny Bobby Shaftoe!

Bobby Shaftoe's young and fair,
Combing down his yellow hair;
He's my love for evermore,
Bonny Bobby Shaftoe!

Bessy Bell and Mary Gray

Bessy Bell and Mary Gray,
They were two bonny lasses;
They built their house upon the lea,
And covered it with rashes.

Bessy kept the garden gate,
And Mary kept the Pantry;
Bessy always had to wait,
While Mary lived in plenty.

A Million Little Diamonds

A million little diamonds
Twinkled on the trees;
And all the little maidens said,
'A jewel, if you please.'
But while they held their hands outstretched,
To catch the diamonds gay,
A million little sunbeams came,
And stole them all away.

The Old Woman who Lived by the Sea

There was an old woman who lived by the sea,
And she was as merry as merry could be.
She did nothing but carol from morning till night,
And sometimes she carolled by candlelight.
She carolled in time and she carolled in tune,
But none cared to hear save the man in the moon.

If Wishes Were Horses

If wishes were horses,
Beggars would ride;
If turnips were watches,
I would wear one by my side.

I Think So, Don't You?

If many men knew what many men know,
If many men went where many men go,
If many men did what many men do,
The world would be better; I think so, don't you?

If muffins and crumpets grew all ready toasted,
And sucking pigs ran about all ready roasted,
And the bushes were covered with jackets all new,
It would be convenient; I think so, don't you?

Thirty Days Hath September

Thirty days hath September,
April, June and November;
All the rest have thirty-one,
Excepting February alone,
And that has twenty-eight days clear
And twenty-nine in each leap year.

Doctor Foster

Doctor Foster went to Gloucester
In a shower of rain;
He stepped in a puddle,
Right up to his middle,
And never went there again.

Peter, Peter, Pumpkin Eater

Peter, Peter, pumpkin eater,
Had a wife and couldn't keep her;
He put her in a pumpkin shell,
And there he kept her very well.

Peter, Peter, pumpkin eater,
Had another but didn't love her;
Peter learned to read and spell,
And then he loved her very well.

An Egg

In marble walls as white as milk,
Lined with a skin as soft as silk,
Within a fountain crystal clear
A golden apple doth appear.
No doors there are to this stronghold,
Yet thieves break in and steal the gold.

The Three Cows

There was an old woman who had three cows –
Rosy and Colin and Dun.
Rosy and Colin were sold at the fair,
And Dun broke her heart in a fit of despair.
So there was an end of her three cows –
Rosy and Colin and Dun.

Molly, My Sister

Molly, my sister, and I fell out,
And what do you think it was all about?
She loved coffee and I loved tea.
And that was the reason we couldn't agree.

Of All the Gay Birds

Of all the gay birds that e'er I did see,
The owl is the fairest by far to me;
For all the day long she sits on a tree,
And when the night comes away flies she.
To-whit, To-whoo,
Sir knave to you,
Her song is well sung, To-whit, To-whoo.

There Was an Old Woman

There was an old woman tossed up in a basket,
Seventeen times as high as the moon;
And where she was going I couldn't but ask it,
For in her hand she carried a broom.

'Old woman, old woman, old woman,' said I,
'O whither, O whither, O whither so high?'
'To sweep the cobwebs off the sky!
And I'll be with you by and by.'

Mary's Lamb

Mary had a little lamb,
Its fleece was white as snow;
And everywhere that Mary went
The lamb was sure to go.

He followed her to school one day;
That was against the rule;
It made the children laugh and play
To see a lamb at school.

And so the teacher turned him out,
But still he lingered near,
And waited patiently about
Till Mary did appear.

'Why does the lamb love Mary so?'
The eager children cry;
'Why, Mary loves the lamb, you know,'
The teacher did reply.

Mary had a little lamb

Mary, Mary

Mary, Mary, quite contrary,
How does your garden grow?
With silver bells and cockle shells,
And pretty maids all in a row.

I Would, if I Could

I would, if I could,
If I couldn't, how could I?
I couldn't, without I could, could I?
Could you, without you could, could ye?
Could ye? could ye?
Could you, without you could, could ye?

Jack Sprat

Jack Sprat could eat no fat,
His wife could eat no lean,
So between them both, you see,
They licked the platter clean.
Jack ate all the lean,
Joan ate all the fat,
The bone they picked it clean,
Then gave it to the cat.

Jack Sprat was wheeling
His wife by the ditch,
The barrow turned over,
And in she did pitch;
Says Jack, 'She'll be drowned,'
But Joan did reply,
'I don't think I shall,
For the ditch is quite dry.'

Elsie Marley

Elsie Marley is grown so fine,
She won't get up to feed the swine,
But lies in bed till eight or nine.
Lazy Elsie Marley.

What Are Little Boys Made Of?

What are little boys made of?
What are little boys made of?
Frogs and snails and puppy-dogs' tails,
That's what little boys are made of.

What are little girls made of?
What are little girls made of?
Sugar and spice and all things nice,
That's what little girls are made of.

Little Betty Blue

Little Betty Blue
Lost her holiday shoe.
What can little Betty do?
Give her another
To match the other,
And then she may walk in two.

Cock a Doodle Doo

Cock a doodle doo!
My dame has lost her shoe;
My master's lost his fiddling stick,
And don't know what to do.

Cock a doodle doo!
What is my dame to do?
Till master finds his fiddling stick,
She'll dance without her shoe.

Cock a doodle doo!
My dame has lost her shoe,
And master's found his fiddling stick;
Sing doodle doodle doo!

Cock a doodle doo!
My dame will dance with you,
While master fiddles his fiddling stick,
For dame and doodle doo.

Cock a doodle doo!
Dame has lost her shoe;
Gone to bed and scratched her head,
And can't tell what to do.

Solomon Grundy

Solomon Grundy,
Born on Monday,
Christened on Tuesday,
Married on Wednesday,
Took ill on Thursday,
Worse on Friday,
Died on Saturday,
Buried on Sunday.
This is the end
Of Solomon Grundy.

Come to the Window

Come to the window,
My baby, with me,
And look at the stars
That shine on the sea.

There are two little stars
That play at bo-peep
With two little fish
Far down in the deep.

And two little frogs
Cry neap, neap, neap;
I see a dear baby
That should be asleep.

London Bridge

London Bridge is falling down,
Falling down, falling down,
London Bridge is falling down,
My fair lady.

How shall we build it up again,
Up again, Up again?
How shall we build it up again?
My fair lady.

Build it up with wood and clay,
Wood and clay, wood and clay,
Build it up with wood and clay,
My fair lady.

Wood and clay will wash away,
Wash away, wash away,
Wood and clay will wash away,
My fair lady.

Build it up with bricks and mortar,
Bricks and mortar, bricks and mortar,
Build it up with bricks and mortar,
My fair lady.

Bricks and mortar will not stay,
Will not stay, will not stay,
Bricks and mortar will not stay,
My fair lady.

Build it up with iron and steel,
Iron and steel, iron and steel,
Build it up with iron and steel,
My fair lady.

Iron and steel will bend and bow,
Bend and bow, bend and bow,
Iron and steel will bend and bow,
My fair lady.

Build it up with silver and gold,
Silver and gold, silver and gold,
Build it up with silver and gold,
My fair lady.

Silver and gold will be stolen away,
Stolen away, stolen away,
Silver and gold will be stolen away,
My fair lady.

Set a man to watch all night,
Watch all night, watch all night,
Set a man to watch all night,
My fair lady.

Suppose the man should fall asleep,
Fall asleep, fall asleep,
Suppose the man should fall asleep?
My fair lady.

Give him a pipe to smoke all night,
Smoke all night, smoke all night,
Give him a pipe to smoke all night,
My fair lady.

My Maid Mary

My maid Mary, she minds her dairy,
While I go hoeing and mowing each morn.
Merrily run the reel,
And the little spinning-wheel,
Whilst I am singing and mowing my corn.

Nuts an' May

Here we come gathering nuts an' may,
Nuts an' may, nuts an' may;
Here we come gathering nuts an' may,
On a fine and frosty morning.

Pray who will you gather for nuts an' may,
Nuts an' may, nuts an' may;
Pray who will you gather for nuts an' may,
On a fine and frosty morning?

We'll gather Sally for nuts an' may,
Nuts an' may, nuts an' may;
We'll gather Sally for nuts an' may,
On a fine and frosty morning.

Who'll you send to take her away,
Take her away, take her away;
Pray who'll you send to take her away,
On a fine and frosty morning?

We'll send Johnny Brown to take her away,
Take her away, take her away;
We'll send Johnny Brown to take her away,
On a fine and frosty morning.

Polly, Put the Kettle On

Polly, put the kettle on,
Polly, put the kettle on,
Polly, put the kettle on,
And let's have tea.

Sukey, take it off again,
Sukey, take it off again,
Sukey, take if off again,
They've all gone away.

I Love Sixpence

I love sixpence, pretty little sixpence,
I love sixpence better than my life;
I spent a penny of it, I spent another,
And I took fourpence home to my wife.

Oh, my little fourpence, pretty little fourpence,
I love fourpence better than my life;
I spent a penny of it, I spent another,
And I took twopence home to my wife.

Oh, my little twopence, pretty little twopence,
I love twopence better than my life;
I spent a penny of it, I spent another,
And I took nothing home to my wife.

Duke of York

Oh, the grand old Duke of York,
He had ten thousand men;
He marched them up to the top of the hill,
And he marched them down again.
And when they were up, they were up,
And when they were down, they were down,
And when they were only half-way up,
They were neither up nor down.

Round and Round the Garden

Round and round the garden
Like a teddy bear;
One step, two step,
Tickle you under there!

Eency, Weency Spider

Eency, weency spider
Climbed the water spout;
Down came the rain
And washed poor spider out.
Out came the sunshine
And dried up the rain.
Eency, weency spider
Climbed up again.

The Little Pig

This little pig went to market,
This little pig stayed at home,
This little pig had roast beef,
This little pig had none,
And this little pig cried,
'Wee-wee-wee-wee-wee,'
All the way home.

Gee Up Neddy

Gee up, Neddy, to the fair;
What shall we buy when we get there?
A penny apple and a penny pear;
Gee up, Neddy, to the fair.

The Farmer in the Dell

The farmer in the dell,
The farmer in the dell,
Heigho, the derry oh,
The farmer in the dell.

The farmer takes a wife,
The farmer takes a wife,
Heigho, the derry oh,
The farmer takes a wife.

The wife takes the child,
The wife takes the child,
Heigho, the derry oh,
The wife takes the child.

The child takes the nurse,
The child takes the nurse,
Heigho, the derry oh,
The child takes the nurse.

The nurse takes the dog,
The nurse takes the dog,
Heigho, the derry oh,
The nurse takes the dog.

The dog takes the cat,
The dog takes the cat,
Heigho, the derry oh,
The dog takes the cat.

The cat takes the rat,
The cat takes the rat,
Heigho, the derry oh,
The cat takes the rat.

The rat takes the cheese,
The rat takes the cheese,
Heigho, the derry oh,
The rat takes the cheese.

The cheese stands alone,
The cheese stands alone,
Heigho, the derry oh,
The cheese stands alone.

Dance to Your Daddie

Dance to your daddie,
My bonnie laddie,
Dance to your daddie, my bonnie lamb;
You shall get a fishie,
On a little dishie,
You shall get a herring when the boat comes hame.

Dance to your daddie,
My bonny laddie,
Dance to your daddie, and to your mammie sing;
You shall get a coatie,
And a pair of breekies,
You shall get a coatie when the boat comes in.

Come, Let's to Bed

'Come, let's to bed,' says Sleepy-head,
'Let's stay awhile,' says Slow,
'Put on the pot,' says Greedy-gut,
'We'll sup before we go.'

There Was a Little Girl

There was a little girl and she had a little curl
Right in the middle of her forehead;
When she was good, she was very, very good,
But when she was bad, she was horrid.

The Mulberry Bush

Here we go round the mulberry bush,
The mulberry bush, the mulberry bush,
Here we go round the mulberry bush,
On a cold and frosty morning.

This is the way we wash our hands,
Wash our hands, wash our hands,
This is the way we wash our hands,
On a cold and frosty morning.

This is the way we wash our clothes,
Wash our clothes, wash our clothes,
This is the way we wash our clothes,
On a cold and frosty morning.

This is the way we go to school,
Go to school, go to school,
This is the way we go to school,
On a cold and frosty morning.

This is the way we come out of school,
Come out of school, come out of school,
This is the way we come out of school,
On a cold and frosty morning.

Old King Cole

Old King Cole was a merry old soul,
And a merry old soul was he;
He called for his pipe, and he called for his bowl,
And he called for his fiddlers three.

Every fiddler, he had a fine fiddle,
And a very fine fiddle had he;
Oh, there's none so rare as can compare
With King Cole and his fiddlers three.

Old Mother Goose

Old Mother Goose,
When she wanted to wander,
Would ride through the air
On a very fine gander.

Mother Goose had a house,
'Twas built in the wood,
And an owl at the door
For sentinel stood.

She had a son Jack,
A plain-looking lad,
He was not very good,
Nor yet very bad.

She sent him to market,
A live goose he bought.
'Here, mother,' says he.
'It will not go for naught.'

Jack's goose and her gander
Grew very fond;
They'd both eat together,
Or swim in one pond.

Jack found one morning,
As I have been told,
His goose had laid him
An egg of pure gold.

Jack sold his gold egg
To a rascally knave;
Not half of its value
To poor Jack he gave.

The knave and the squire
Came up at his back,
And began to belabour
The sides of poor Jack.

And then the gold egg
Was thrown into the sea,
When Jack he jumped in,
And got it back presently.

And Old Mother Goose,
The goose saddled soon,
And mounting its back,
Flew up to the moon.

O Dear, What Can the Matter Be?

O dear, what can the matter be?
Dear, dear, what can the matter be?
O dear, what can the matter be?
Johnny's so long at the fair.

He promised he'd bring me a fairing to please me,
And then for a kiss, oh, he vowed he would tease me,
He promised he'd buy me a bunch of blue ribbons
To tie up my bonny brown hair.

And it's O dear, what can the matter be?
Dear, dear, what can the matter be?
O dear, what can the matter be?
Johnny's so long at the fair.

He promised to bring me a pair of sleeve buttons,
A pair of new garters that cost him but twopence,
He promised he'd buy me a bunch of blue ribbons
To tie up my bonny brown hair.

And it's O dear, what can the matter be?
Dear, dear, what can the matter be?
O dear, what can the matter be?
Johnny's so long at the fair.

He promised he'd bring me a basket of posies,
A garland of lilies, a garland of roses,
A little straw hat, to set off the ribbons
That tie up my bonny brown hair.

Lavender's Blue

Lavender's blue, dilly dilly,
Lavender's green,
When I am king, dilly dilly,
You shall be queen.
Who told you so, dilly dilly,
Who told you so?
'Twas mine own heart, dilly dilly,
That told me so.

Call up your men, dilly dilly,
Set them to work,
Some with a rake, dilly dilly,
Some with a fork;
Some to make hay, dilly dilly,
Some to thresh corn,
Whilst you and I, dilly, dilly,
Keep ourselves warm.

If you should die, dilly dilly,
As it may hap,
You shall be buried, dilly dilly,
Under the tap.
Who told you so, dilly dilly,
Pray tell me why?
That you might drink, dilly dilly,
When you are dry.

Hickety, Pickety

Hickety, pickety, my fine hen,
She lays eggs for gentlemen;
Gentlemen come every day
To see what my fine hen doth lay.
Sometimes nine and sometimes ten,
Hickety, pickety, my fine hen.

A Little Guinea-pig

There was a little guinea-pig,
Who, being little, was not big;
He always walked upon his feet,
And never fasted when he ate.

When from a place he ran away,
He never at that place did stay;
And while he ran, as I am told,
He ne'er stood still for young or old.

He often squeaked and sometimes vi'lent;
And when he squeaked he ne'er was silent;
Though ne'er instructed by a cat,
He knew a mouse was not a rat.

One day, as I am certified,
He took a whim and fairly died;
And, as I'm told by men of sense,
He never has been living since.

Pop Goes the Weasel

Up and down the City Road,
In and out of the Eagle,
That's the way the money goes,
Pop goes the weasel!

Half a pound of tuppenny rice,
Half a pound of treacle,
Mix it up and make it nice,
Pop goes the weasel!

Every night when I go out
The monkey's on the table;
Take a stick and knock it off,
Pop goes the weasel!

The Muffin Man

O do you know the muffin man,
The muffin man, the muffin man,
O do you know the muffin man,
That lives in Drury Lane?

O yes, I know the muffin man,
The muffin man, the muffin man,
O yes, I know the muffin man,
That lives in Drury Lane.

Ten Little Injuns

Ten little Injuns standing in a line,
One went home, and then there were nine.

Nine little Injuns swinging on a gate,
One tumbled off, and then there were eight.

Eight little Injuns gayest under heaven,
One kicked the bucket, and then there were seven.

Seven little Injuns cutting up tricks,
One broke his neck, and then there were six.

Six little Injuns kicking all alive,
One went to bed, and then there were five.

Five little Injuns on a cellar door,
One tumbled off, and then there were four.

Four little Injuns climbing up a tree,
One fell down, and then there were three.

Three little Injuns out in a canoe,
One tumbled overboard, and then there were two.

Two little Injuns fooling with a gun,
One shot the other, and then there was one.

One little Injun living all alone,
He got married, and then there was none!

The Old Woman Who Lived in a Shoe

There was an old woman who lived in a shoe,
She had so many children she didn't know what to do.
She gave them some broth without any bread;
She whipped them all soundly and put them to bed.

Oranges and Lemons

Gay go up, and gay go down
To ring the bells of London Town.

Bull's eyes and targets,
Say the bells of St Margaret's.

Brickbats and tiles,
Say the bells of St Giles'.

Pancakes and fritters,
Say the bells of St Peter's.

Two sticks and an apple,
Say the bells at Whitechapel.

Halfpence and farthings,
Say the bells of St Martin's.

Oranges and lemons,
Say the bells of St Clement's.

Old Father Baldpate,
Say the slow bells at Aldgate.

Pokers and tongs,
Say the bells of St John's.

Kettles and pans,
Say the bells of St Ann's.

You owe me ten shillings,
Say the bells at St Helen's.

When will you pay me?
Say the bells at Old Bailey.

When I grow rich,
Say the bells at Shoreditch.

Pray when will that be?
Say the bells of Stepney.

I am sure I don't know,
Says the great bell of Bow.

Here comes a candle to light you to bed,
And here comes a chopper to chop off your head.

An Owl

In an oak there lived an owl,
Frisky, whisky, wheedle!
She thought herself a clever fowl;
Fiddle, faddle, feedle.

Her face alone her wisdom shew,
Frisky, whisky, wheedle!
For all she said was, 'Whit te whoo!'
Fiddle, faddle, feedle.

Her silly note a gunner heard,
Frisky, whisky, wheedle!
Says he, 'I'll shoot you, stupid bird!'
Fiddle, Faddle, Feedle.

Now if he had not heard her hoot,
Frisky, whisky, wheedle,
He had not found her out to shoot,
Fiddle, faddle, feedle.

Wouldn't It Be Funny?

Wouldn't it be funny,
Wouldn't it now,
If the dog said, 'Moo-oo'
And the cow said, 'Bow-wow?'
If the cat sang and whistled,
And the bird said, 'Mia-ow?'
Wouldn't it be funny,
Wouldn't it now?

There Was a Monkey

There was a monkey climbed up a tree,
When he fell down, then down fell he.

There was a crow sat on a stone,
When he was gone, then there was none.

There was an old wife did eat an apple,
When she ate two, she ate a couple.

There was a horse going to the mill,
When he went on, he stood not still.

There was a butcher cut his thumb,
When it did bleed, then blood did come.

There was a lackey ran a race,
When he ran fast, he ran apace.

There was a cobbler clouting shoon,
When they were mended, they were done.

There was a chandler making candle,
When he them stripped, he did them handle.

There was a navy went to Spain,
When it returned, it came again.

Jenny Wren and Robin Redbreast

Jenny Wren fell sick
Upon a merry time,
In came Robin Redbreast
And brought her cake and wine.

'Eat well of the cake, Jenny,
Drink well of the wine.'
'Thank you, Robin, kindly,
You shall be mine.'

Jenny Wren got well,
And stood upon her feet;
And told Robin plainly,
She loved him not a bit.

Robin, he was angry,
And hopped upon a twig,
Saying, 'Out upon you, fie upon you!
Bold faced jig!'

There Was an Old Woman

There was an old woman lived under a hill;
And if she's not gone, she lives there still.
Baked apples she sold, and cranberry pies,
And she's the old woman who never told lies.

A Little Pig

A little pig found a fifty-pound note
And purchased a hat and a very fine coat,
With trousers, and stockings, and shoes,
Cravat, and shirt-collar, and gold-headed cane;
Then proud as could be, did he march up the lane,
Says he, 'I shall hear all the news.'

Three Little Kittens

Three little kittens, they lost their mittens,
And they began to cry,
'Oh, mother dear, we sadly fear
That we have lost our mittens.'

'What! Lost your mittens, You naughty kittens!
Then you shall have no pie.
Mee-ow, mee-ow, mee-ow.
No, you shall have no pie.'

The three little kittens, they found their mittens,
And they began to cry,
'Oh, mother dear, see here, see here,
For we have found our mittens.'

'What! Found your mittens, you silly kittens!
Then you shall have some pie.
Purr-r, purr-r, purr-r,
Oh, let us have some pie.'

Three little kittens, put on their mittens,
And soon ate up the pie;
'Oh, mother dear, we greatly fear
That we have soiled our mittens.'

'What! Soiled your mittens, you naughty kittens!'
Then they began to sigh,
'Mee-ow, mee-ow, mee-ow.'
Then they began to sigh.

The three little kittens they washed their mittens,
And hung them out to dry;
'Oh, mother dear, do you not hear,
That we have washed our mittens?'

'What! Washed your mittens? you're good little kittens.
But I smell a rat close by.
Mee-ow, mee-ow, mee-ow.
I smell a rat close by.'

Six Little Mice

Six little mice sat down to spin;
Pussy passed by and she peeped in.
'What are you doing, my little men?'
'Weaving coats for gentlemen.'
'Shall I come in and cut off your threads?'
'No, no, Mistress Pussy, you'd bite off our heads.'
'Oh, no, I'll not; I'll help you to spin.'
'That may be so, but you don't come in.'

See-Saw, Margery Daw

See-saw, Margery Daw,
Johnny shall have a new master;
He shall have but a penny a day,
Because he can't work any faster.

Simple Simon

Simple Simon met a pieman,
Going to the fair;
Says Simple Simon to the pieman,
'Let me taste your ware.'

Says the pieman to Simple Simon,
'Show me first your penny.'
Says Simple Simon to the pieman,
'Indeed I have not any.'

Simple Simon went a-fishing,
For to catch a whale;
All the water he had got
Was in his mother's pail.

He went to catch a dickie bird,
And thought he could not fail,
Because he'd got a little salt,
To put upon his tail.

Simple Simon went a-hunting,
For to catch a hare;
He rode an ass about the streets,
But couldn't find one there.

Once Simon made a great snowball,
And brought it home to roast;
He laid it down before the fire,
And soon the ball was lost.

He went to slide upon the ice,
Before the ice would bear;
Then he plunged in above his knees,
Which made poor Simon stare.

Simple Simon went to look
If plums grew on a thistle;
He pricked his fingers very much,
Which made poor Simon whistle.

He went for water in a sieve,
But soon it all ran through.
And now poor Simple Simon
Bids you all adieu.

I Had a Cat

I had a cat and the cat pleased me,
I fed my cat by yonder tree;
Cat goes, 'Fiddle-i-fee.'

I had a hen and the hen pleased me,
I fed my hen by yonder tree;
Hen goes, 'Chimmy-chuck, chimmy-chuck,'
Cat goes, 'Fiddle-i-fee.'

I had a duck and the duck pleased me,
I fed my duck by yonder tree;
Duck goes, 'Quack, quack,'
Hen goes, 'Chimmy-chuck, chimmy-chuck,'
Cat goes, 'Fiddle-i-fee.'

I had a goose and the goose pleased me,
I fed my goose by yonder tree;
Goose goes, 'Swishy, swashy,'
Duck goes, 'Quack, quack,'
Hen goes, 'Chimmy-chuck, chimmy-chuck,'
Cat goes, 'Fiddle-i-fee.'

I had a sheep and the sheep pleased me,
I fed my sheep by yonder tree;
Sheep goes, 'Baa, baa,'
Goose goes, 'Swishy, swashy,'
Duck goes, 'Quack, quack,'
Hen goes, 'Chimmy-chuck, chimmy-chuck,'
Cat goes, 'Fiddle-i-fee.'

I had a pig and the pig pleased me,
I fed my pig by yonder tree;
Pig goes, 'Griffy, gruffy,'
Sheep goes, 'Baa, baa,'
Goose goes, 'Swishy, swashy,'
Duck goes, 'Quack, quack,'
Hen goes, 'Chimmy-chuck, chimmy-chuck,'
Cat goes, 'Fiddle-i-fee.'

I had a cow and the cow pleased me,
I fed my cow by yonder tree;
Cow goes, 'Moo, moo,'
Pig goes, 'Griffy, gruffy,'
Sheep goes, 'Baa, baa,'
Goose goes, 'Swishy, swashy,'
Duck goes, 'Quack, quack,'
Hen goes, 'Chimmy-chuck, chimmy-chuck,'
Cat goes, 'Fiddle-i-fee.'

I had a horse and the horse pleased me,
I fed my horse by yonder tree;
Horse goes, 'Neigh, neigh,'
Cow goes, 'Moo, moo,'
Pig goes, 'Griffy, gruffy,'
Sheep goes, 'Baa, baa,'
Goose goes, 'Swishy, swashy,'
Duck goes, 'Quack, quack,'
Hen goes, 'Chimmy-chuck, chimmy-chuck,'
Cat goes, 'Fiddle-i-fee.'

I had a dog and the dog pleased me,
I fed my dog by yonder tree;
Dog goes, 'Bow-wow, bow-wow,'
Horse goes, 'Neigh, neigh,'
Cow goes, 'Moo, moo,'
Pig goes, 'Griffy, gruffy,'
Sheep goes, 'Baa, baa,'
Goose goes, 'Swishy, swashy,'
Duck goes, 'Quack, quack,'
Hen goes, 'Chimmy-chuck, chimmy-chuck,'
Cat goes, 'Fiddle-i-fee.'

A Walnut

As soft as silk, as white as milk,
As bitter as gall, a thick wall
And a green coat cover me all.

A Jolly Miller

There was a jolly miller once,
Lived on the river Dee;
He worked and sang from morn till night,
No lark more blithe than he.
And this the burden of his song
Forever used to be,
'I care for nobody, no! not I,
If nobody cares for me.'

Three Jovial Welshmen

There were three jovial Welshmen,
As I have heard them say,
And they would go a-hunting
Upon St David's day.

All the day they hunted,
And nothing could they find
But a ship a-sailing,
A-sailing with the wind.

One said it was a ship,
The other he said, nay;
The third said it was a house,
With the chimney blown away.

And all the night they hunted,
And nothing could they find
But the moon a-gliding,
A-gliding with the wind.

One said it was the moon,
The other he said, nay;
The third said it was a cheese,
And half of it cut away.

And all the day they hunted,
And nothing could they find
But a hedgehog in a bramble bush,
And that they left behind.

The first said it was a hedgehog,
The second he said, nay;
The third it was a pin-cushion,
And the pins stuck in wrong way.

And all the night they hunted,
And nothing could they find
But a hare in a turnip field,
And that they left behind.

The first said it was a hare,
The second he said, nay;
The third said it was a calf,
And the cow had run away.

And all the day they hunted,
And nothing could they find
But an owl in a holly tree,
And that they left behind.

One said it was an owl,
The other he said, nay,
The third said 'twas an old man,
Whose his beard was growing grey.

Sing a Song of Sixpence

Sing a song of sixpence,
A pocket full of rye;
Four-and-twenty blackbirds,
Baked in a pie.

When the pie was opened,
The birds began to sing;
Was not that a dainty dish,
To set before the king?

The king was in his counting-house,
Counting out his money;
The queen was in the parlour,
Eating bread and honey.

The maid was in the garden,
Hanging out the clothes,
When down came a blackbird,
And pecked off her nose.

Sing a
Song of Sixpence.

The babes
in the wood

The Babes in the Wood

My dear, do you know
How a long time ago
Two poor little children,
Whose names I don't know,
Were stolen away
On a fine summer's day,
And left in a wood,
As I've heard people say.

And when it was night,
So sad was their plight,
The sun it went down,
And the moon gave no light!
They sobbed and they sighed,
And they bitterly cried,
And the poor little things
They laid down and died.

And when they were dead,
The robins so red
Brought strawberry leaves,
And over them spread;
And all the day long,
They sang them this song,
Poor babes in the wood!
Poor babes in the wood!
And don't you remember
The babes in the wood?

The Spider and The Fly

'Will you walk into my parlour?'
Said the spider to the fly.
' 'Tis the prettiest little parlour
That ever you did spy.
The way into my parlour
Is up a winding stair;
And I have many curious things
To show you when you're there.'
'Oh, no, no,' said the little fly;
'To ask me is in vain;
For who goes up your winding stair
Can ne'er come down again.'

'I'm sure you must be weary, dear,
With soaring up so high;
Will you rest upon my little bed?'
Said the spider to the fly.
'There are pretty curtains drawn around;
The sheets are fine and thin;
And if you like to rest awhile,
I'll snugly tuck you in!'
'Oh, no, no,' said the little fly;
'For I've often heard it said,
They never, never wake again
Who sleep upon your bed!'

Said the cunning spider to the fly,
'Dear friend, what can I do
To prove the warm affection
I've always felt for you?'
'I thank you, gentle sir,' she said,
'For what you're pleased to say,
And bidding you good-morning now,
I'll call another day.'

The spider turned him round about,
And went into his den,
For well he knew the silly fly
Would soon come back again;
So he wove a subtle web
In a little corner sly,
And set his table ready
To dine upon the fly.
Then he came out to his door again,
And, merrily did sing,
'Come hither, hither, pretty fly,
With the pearl and silver wing;
Your robes are green and purple,
There's a crest upon your head.
Your eyes are like the diamond bright,
But mine are dull as lead!'

Alas! alas! how very soon
This silly little fly,
Hearing his wily, flattering words,
Came slowly flitting by.
With buzzing wings she hung aloft,
Then near and nearer drew,
Thinking only of her brilliant eyes,
Her green and purple hue,
Thinking only of her crested head,
Poor foolish thing! At last,
Up jumped the cunning spider,
And fiercely held her fast!
He dragged her up his winding stair,
Into his dismal den
Within his little parlour,
But she ne'er came out again!

And now, dear little children,
Who may this story read,
To idle, silly, flattering words,
I pray you ne'er give heed;
Unto an evil counsellor
Close heart and ear and eye,
And take a lesson from this tale
Of the Spider and the Fly.

I Saw Three Ships

I saw three ships come sailing by,
Come sailing by, come sailing by,
I saw three ships come sailing by,
On New Year's Day in the morning.

And what do you think was in them then,
Was in them then, was in them then?
And what do you think was in them then,
On New Year's Day in the morning?

Three pretty girls were in them then,
Were in them then, were in them then,
Three pretty girls were in them then,
On New Year's Day in the morning.

One could whistle, and one could sing,
And one could play on the violin;
Such joy there was at my wedding,
On New Year's Day in the morning.

How Many Miles to Babylon?

'How many miles is it to Babylon?'
'Threescore miles and ten.'
'Can I get there by candle-light?'
'Yes, and back again.
If your heels are nimble and light,
You may get there by candle-light.'

Roses Are Red

Roses are red,
Lavender's blue;
If you will have me,
I will have you.

Lilies are white,
Rosemary's green;
When you are king,
I will be queen.

King Pippin

Little King Pippin, he built a fine hall.
Pie-crust and pastry-crust, that was the wall;
The windows were made of
Black puddings and white;
The roof was of pancakes –
You ne'er saw the like.

I Had a Little Moppet

I had a little moppet,
I put it in my pocket,
And fed it with corn and hay;
Then came a proud beggar,
And swore he would have her,
And stole little moppet away.

A was an Archer

A was an Archer, who shot at a frog.
B was a Butcher, who had a great dog.
C was a Captain, all covered with lace.
D was a Dunce, with a very sad face.
E was an Esquire, with pride on his brow.
F was a Farmer, who followed the plough.
G was a Gamester, who had but ill luck.
H was a Hunter, who hunted a buck.
I was an Innkeeper, who loved to carouse,
J was a Joiner, who built up a house.
K was a King, so mighty and grand.
L was a Lady, who had a white hand.
M was a Miser, who hoarded up gold.
N was a Nobleman, gallant and bold.
O was an Oysterman, who went about town.
P was a Parson, who wore a black gown.
Q was a Quack, with a wonderful pill.
R was a Robber, who wanted to kill.
S was a Sailor, who spent all he got.
T was a Tinker, who mended a pot.
U was a Usurer, a miserable elf.
V was a Vintner, who drank all himself.
W was a Watchman, who guarded the door.
X was Expensive, and so became poor.
Y was a Youth, that did not love school.
Z was a Zany, a poor harmless fool.

The Cat and the Fiddle

Hey-diddle-diddle,
The cat and the fiddle,
The cow jumped over the moon;
The little dog laughed
To see such sport,
And the dish ran away with the spoon.

Hey-diddle-diddle,
the Cat
and the Fiddle.

Old Mother Hubbard

Old Mother Hubbard
Went to the cupboard
To get her poor dog a bone;
But when she came there
The cupboard was bare,
And so the poor dog had none.

She went to the baker's
To buy him some bread;
But when she came back
The poor dog was dead.

She went to the undertaker's
To buy him a coffin;
But when she came back
The poor dog was laughing.

She took a clean dish
To get him some tripe;
But when she came back
He was smoking his pipe.

She went to the fruiterer's
To buy him some fruit;
But when she came back
He was playing the flute.

She went to the barber's
To buy him a wig;
But when she came back
He was dancing a jig.

She went to the tailor's
To buy him a coat;
But when she came back
He was riding a goat.

She went to the hatter's
To buy him a hat;
But when she came back
He was feeding the cat.

She went to the cobbler's
To buy him some shoes;
But when she came back
He was reading the news.

She went to the seamstress
To buy him some linen;
But when she came back
The dog was a-spinning.

The damme made a curtsy,
The dog made a bow;
The dame said, 'Your servant,,'
The dog said, 'Bow-wow.'

Good King Arthur

When good King Arthur ruled this land
He was a goodly king:
He took three pecks of barley meal
To make a bag pudding.

A rare pudding the king did make,
And stuffed it well with plums;
And in it put great lumps of fat,
As big as my two thumbs.

The king and queen sat down to dine,
And noblemen beside;
And what they could not eat that night
The queen next morning fried.

One, Two, Buckle My Shoe

One, two, buckle my shoe,
Three, four, shut the door,
Five, six, pick up sticks,
Seven, eight, lay them straight,
Nine, ten, a good fat hen,
Eleven, twelve, dig and delve,
Thirteen, fourteen, maids are courting,
fifteen, sixteen, maids in the kitchen,
Seventeen, eighteen, maids are waiting,
Nineteen, twenty, my plate's empty.

Humpty Dumpty

Humpty Dumpty sat on a wall,
Humpty Dumpty had a great fall;
All the king's horses and all the king's men
Couldn't put Humpty together again.

Willy Boy, Willy Boy

Willy boy, Willy boy, where are you going?
I will go with you, if that I may.
I'm going to the meadow to see them a-mowing,
I'm going to help them to make the hay.

One, Two, Three, Four, Five

One, two, three, four, five,
Once I caught a fish alive.
Six, seven, eight, nine, ten,
Then I let it go again.
Why did you let it go?
Because it bit my finger so.
Which finger did it bite?
The little finger on the right.

Ladybird

Ladybird, Ladybird,
Fly away home;
Your house is on fire,
And your children are gone;
All except one,
And her name is Ann,
And she has crept under
The pudding pan.

Fe, Fi, Fo, Fum

Fe, Fi, Fo, Fum!
I smell the blood of an Englishman;
Be he alive or be he dead,
I'll grind his bones to make my bread.

The Bumble Bee

The bumble bee, the bumble bee,
He flew to the top of the tulip tree;
He flew to the top, but he could not stop,
For he had to get home to early tea.

The bumble bee, the bumble bee,
He flew away from the tulip tree;
But he made a mistake and flew into a lake,
And he never got home to early tea.

Three Young Rats

Three young rats with black felt hats,
Three young ducks with white straw flats,
Three young dogs with curling tails,
Three young cats with demi-veils,
Went out to walk with two young pigs
In satin vests and sorrel wigs;
But suddenly it chanced to rain,
And so they all went home again.

I Had a Little Nut-tree

I had a little nut-tree, nothing would it bear
But a silver nutmeg and a golden pear;
The King of Spain's daughter came to visit me,
And all was because of my little nut-tree.
I skipped over water, I danced over sea,
And all the birds in the air couldn't catch me.

Diddle, Diddle, Dumpling

Diddle, diddle, dumpling, my son John,
Went to bed with his trousers on;
One shoe off and one shoe on;
Diddle, diddle, dumpling, my son John.

To Market, To Market

To market, to market to buy a fat pig,
Home again, home again, jiggety-jig;
To market, to market to buy a fat hog,
Home again, home again, jiggety-jog.

Hector Protector

Hector Protector was dressed all in green;
Hector Protector was sent to the queen.
The queen did not like him,
No more did the king;
So Hector Protector was sent back again.

Little Robin Redbreast

Little Robin Redbreast sat upon a tree,
Up went pussy cat, and down went he;
Down came pussy, and away Robin ran;
Says little Robin Redbreast, 'Catch me if you can.'
Little Robin Redbreast jumped upon a wall,
Pussy cat jumped after him, and almost got a fall;
Little Robin chirped and sang, and what did pussy say?
Pussy cat said, 'Mew,' and Robin jumped away.

The Queen of Hearts

The Queen of Hearts, she made some tarts,
All on a summer's day;
The Knave of Hearts, he stole the tarts,
And took them clean away.

The King of Hearts called for the tarts,
And beat the Knave full sore;
The Knave of Hearts brought back the tarts,
And vowed he'd steal no more.

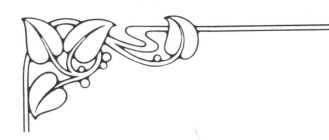

Tom, Tom, the Piper's Son

Tom, Tom, the piper's son,
Stole a pig, and away he run.
The pig was eat, and Tom was beat,
And Tom went roaring down the street.

Two Little Dickie-birds

Two little dickie-birds,
Sitting on a wall,
One named Peter,
The other named Paul;
Fly away, Peter!
Fly away, Paul!
Come back, Peter!
Come back, Paul!

Yankee Doodle

Yankee Doodle came to town,
Riding on a pony;
He stuck a feather in his cap
And called it macaroni.

The Lion and The Unicorn

The lion and the unicorn
Were fighting for the crown;
The lion beat the unicorn
All around the town.
Some gave them white bread,
And some gave them brown;
Some gave them plum cake
And drummed them out of town.

A King and His Daughters

There was a King and he had three daughters,
And they all lived in a basin of water;
The basin bended,
My story's ended.
If the basin had been stronger
My story would have been longer.

Three Blind Mice

Three blind mice. Three blind mice.
See how they run! See how they run!
They all run after the farmer's wife,
Who cut off their tails with a carving knife.
Did you ever see such a thing in your life,
As three blind mice?

I Love Little Pussy

I love little pussy, her coat is so warm,
And if I don't hurt her, she'll do me no harm.
So I'll not pull her tail, nor drive her away,
But pussy and I very gently will play.
I'll sit by the fire, and give her some food,
And pussy will love me because I am good.

The Cuckoo

In April, come he will.
In May, sing all day.
In June, change his tune.
In July, prepare to fly.
In August, go he must!

I Had a Little Pony

I had a little pony,
His name was Dapple Gray,
I lent him to a lady,
To ride a mile away.

She whipped him, she lashed him,
She rode him through the mire;
I would not lend my pony now
For all the lady's hire.

Tommy Snooks and Bessy Brooks

As Tommy Snooks and Bessy Brooks
Were walking out one Sunday,
Says Tommy Snooks to Bessie Brooks,
Wilt marry me on Monday?

Doctor Fell

I do not like thee, Doctor Fell,
The reason why I cannot tell;
But this I know, and know full well,
I do not like thee, Doctor Fell.

Queen Anne

Queen Anne, Queen Anne, you sit in the sun,
As fair as a lily, as white as a swan.
I send you three letters, and pray read one,
You must read one, if you can't read all,
So pray, Miss or Master, throw up the ball.

A Little Cock Sparrow

A little cock sparrow sat on a tree,
Looking as happy as happy could be,
Till a boy came by with his bow and arrow,
Says he, 'I will shoot the little cock sparrow.'

'His body will make me a nice little stew,
And his giblets will make me a little pie too.'
Says the little cock sparrow, 'I'll be shot if I stay,'
So he clapped his wings and flew away.

Where, O Where

Where, O where, has my little dog gone?
O where, O where, can he be?

With his tail cut short, and his ears cut long,
O where, O where, has he gone?

I Need Not Your Needles

I need not your needles,
They're needless to me,
For kneading of needles
Were needless, you see;
But did my neat trousers
But need to be kneed,
I then should have need
Of your needles indeed.

Good-morrow to You, Valentine!

Good-morrow to you, Valentine!
Curl your locks as I do mine;
Two before and three behind;
Good-morrow to you, Valentine!

Ring-a-ring O' Roses

Ring-a-ring o' roses,
A pocket full of posies,
A-tishoo! A-tishoo!
We all fall down.

Snail, Snail

Snail, snail, come out of your hole,
Or else I'll beat you as black as coal.
Snail, snail, put out your horns,
I'll give you bread and barley corns.

Eeny, Meeny

Eeny, meeny, miny, mo,
Catch a beggar by his toe;
If he hollers, let him go,
Eeny, meeny, miny, mo.

Pussy Cat, Pussy Cat

Pussy cat, pussy cat, where have you been?
I've been to London to look at the queen.
Pussy cat, pussy cat, what did you there?
I frightened a little mouse under her chair.

This Old Man

This old man, he played one,
He played knick-knack on my drum,
Knick-knack, paddy whack, give a dog a bone
This old man came rolling home.

This old man, he played two,
He played knick-knack on my shoe,
Knick-knack, paddy whack, give a dog a bone,
This old man came rolling home.

This old man, he played three,
He played knick-knack on my knee,
Knick-knack, paddy whack, give a dog a bone,
This old man came rolling home.

This old man, he played four,
He played knick-knack on my door,
Knick-knack, paddy whack, give a dog a bone,
This old man came rolling home.

This old man, he played five,
He played knick-knack on my hive,
Knick-knack, paddy whack, give a dog a bone,
This old man came rolling home.

This old man, he played six,
He played knick-knack on my sticks,
Knick-knack, paddy whack, give a dog a bone,
This old man came rolling home.

This old man, he played seven,
He played knick-knack on my Devon,
Knick-knack, paddy whack, give a dog a bone,
This old man came rolling home.

This old man, he played eight,
He played knick-knack on my gate,
Knick-knack, paddy whack, give a dog a bone,
This old man came rolling home.

This old man, he played nine,
He played knick-knack on my line,
Knick-knack, paddy whack, give a dog a bone,
This old man came rolling home.

This old man, he played ten,
He played knick-knack on my hen,
Knick-knack, paddy whack, give a dog a bone,
This old man came rolling home.

If I Had a Donkey

If I had a donkey that wouldn't go,
Would I beat him? Oh no, no.
I'd put him in the barn and give him some corn,
The best little donkey that ever was born.

Hot Cross Buns

Hot-cross Buns!
Hot-cross Buns!
One a penny, two a penny,
Hot-cross Buns!

Hot-cross Buns!
Hot-cross Buns!
If you have no daughters
Give them to your sons.

Two Cats of Kilkenny

There were once two cats of Kilkenny,
Each thought there was one cat too many;
So they fought and they fit,
And they scratched and they bit,
Till, excepting their nails
And the tips of their tails,
Instead of two cats, there weren't any!

A Wise Old Owl

A wise old owl lived in an oak;
The more he saw the less he spoke;
The less he spoke the more he heard.
Why can't we be like that wise old bird?

List of Tile Pictures with Artists and Location

M.E.T. = Margaret Thompson (at Doulton from *c.* 1889 to *c.* 1926)
W.R. = William Rowe (at Doulton from 1882 to 1939)
J.H.Mc. = John H. McLennan (at Doulton from 1879 to 1910)
Un. = Unknown

Jacket: *Little Girl, Little Girl*. Artist: M.E.T., Buchanan Hospital, St. Leonard's-on-Sea.

Frontispiece: *Little Miss Muffet*. Artist: M.E.T., Wellington Hospital, Wellington, New Zealand.

Page 11: *Baa, Baa, Black Sheep*. Artist: M.E.T. The Royal Victoria Infirmary, Newcastle-upon-Tyne.

Page 12: *Bless You, Bless You, Burnie Bee*. Artists: W.R. and J.H.Mc. The Royal Victoria Infirmary, Newcastle-upon-Tyne.

Page 21: *Blow, Wind, Blow*. Artist: M.E.T. Buchanan Hospital, St. Leonard's-on-Sea.

Page 22: *Daffy-Down-Dilly*. Artists: W.R. and J.H.Mc. The Royal Victoria Infirmary, Newcastle-upon-Tyne.

Page 31: *Ding, Dong, Bell*. Artists: W.R. and J.H.Mc. The Royal Victoria Infirmary, Newcastle-upon-Tyne.

Page 32: *Goosey, Goosey Gander*. Artist: M.E.T. Buchanan Hospital, St. Leonard's-on-Sea.

Page 41: *Hark, Hark*. Artist: M.E.T. The Royal Victoria Infirmary, Newcastle-upon-Tyne.

Page 42: *Hickory, Dickory, Dock*. Artists: W.R. and J.H.Mc. The Royal Victoria Infirmary, Newcastle-upon-Tyne.

Page 51: *Hush-a-bye Baby*. Artist: M.E.T. The Royal Victoria Infirmary, Newcastle-upon-Tyne.

Page 52: *I Had a Little Husband*. Artist: M.E.T. The Royal Victoria Infirmary, Newcastle-upon-Tyne.

Page 61: *I Saw a Ship A-sailing*. Artist: M.E.T. Buchanan Hospital, St. Leonard's-on-Sea.

Page 62: *Jack and Jill*. Artist: Un. St. Thomas' Hospital, London.

Page 71: *Little Bo-Peep*. Artist: Un. St. Thomas' Hospital, London.

Page 72: *Little Boy Blue*. Artist: M.E.T. Buchanan Hospital, St. Leonard's-on-Sea.

Page 89: *Mary's Lamb*. Artist: M.E.T. Buchanan Hospital, St. Leonard's-on-Sea.

Page 90: *Mary, Mary*. Artist: M.E.T. Wellington Hospital, Wellington, New Zealand.

Page 99: *My Maid Mary*. Artist: M.E.T. The Royal Victoria Infirmary, Newcastle-upon-Tyne.

Page 100: *Nuts an' May*. Artist: M.E.T. Wellington Hospital, Wellington, New Zealand

Page 109: *Old King Cole*. Artist: M.E.T. Wellington Hospital, Wellington, New Zealand.

Page 110: *Old Mother Goose*. Artists: W.R. and J.H.Mc. The Royal Victoria Infirmary, Newcastle-upon-Tyne.

Page 119: *The Old Woman Who Lived in a Shoe*. Artist: M.E.T. The Royal Victoria Infirmary, Newcastle-upon-Tyne.

Page 120: *Oranges and Lemons*. Artist: M.E.T. Buchanan Hospital, St. Leonard's-on-Sea.

Page 129: *See-Saw, Margery Daw*. Artist: M.E.T. Wellington Hospital, Wellington, New Zealand.

Page 130. *Simple Simon*. Artists: W.R. and J.H.Mc. The Royal Victoria Infirmary, Newcastle-upon-Tyne.
Page 139: *Sing a Song of Sixpence*. Artist: M.E.T. Wellington Hospital, Wellington, New Zealand.
Page 140: *The Babes in the Wood*. Artist: Un. St. Thomas' Hospital, London.
Page 149: *The Cat and the Fiddle*. Artist: M.E.T. Wellington Hospital, Wellington, New Zealand.

Page 150: *Old Mother Hubbard*. Artist: M.E.T. The Royal Victoria Infirmary, Newcastle-upon-Tyne.
Page 159: *The Queen of Hearts*. Artist: M.E.T. The Royal Victoria Infirmary, Newcastle-upon-Tyne.
Page 160: *Tom, Tom, the Piper's Son*. Artists: W.R. and J.H.Mc. The Royal Victoria Infirmary, Newcastle-upon-Tyne.

Publishers' Acknowledgements

The Publishers gratefully acknowledge the help and co-operation of Royal Doulton, who designed and manufactured the tiles illustrated in this book.

The Publishers gratefully acknowledge the following, for the valuable assistance given in obtaining the photographs of the tile sets: Bill Black, ex-Publications Officer with the Wellington Hospital Board and the staff of the children's ward, The Wellington Hospital, Wellington, New Zealand; The Royal Victoria Infirmary, Newcastle-upon-Tyne; Hastings Health Authority and Buchanan Hospital, St. Leonard's-on-Sea; and The Special Trustees and staff of St. Thomas' Hospital, London.

Illustration Acknowledgements

Newnes Books, Feltham, Middlesex pages 11, 12, 22, 31, 41, 51, 52, 99, 110, 119, 150, 159, 160
Nova Pacifica Publishing Company, Wellington, New Zealand front jacket, frontispiece, pages 21, 32, 42, 61, 62, 71, 72, 89, 90, 100, 109, 120, 129, 130, 139, 140, 149.

Index of First Lines